This

Little Blue

book belongs to

....

Little Blue

Goes Out to Play

Written by

Margaret Ryan

Illustrated by

Andy Ellis

Hodder
Children's
Books

A division of Hodder Headline Limited

For Jillian
with love
M.R.

For Diana Klemin
with love
A.E.

It was a very wet day.

Little Blue opened the door of

the upturned boat where he lived

and poked out his head.

PLOP PLIP **PLOP, PLOP** PLIP **PLOP.**

Fat raindrops bounced off

his beak. Little Blue sighed.

He wanted to go out and play

with his ball, but it was too wet.

"I know, I'll try out my rain
chant," he said. "Then maybe
the rain will go away."
And he chanted...
"RAIN RAIN GO AWAY, THEN
I CAN GO OUT AND PLAY."
PLOP PLIP **PLOP, PLOP** PLIP **PLOP.**
The rain didn't go away.

"I'll just have to play
with my ball indoors instead,"
said Little Blue.
First he bounced it off the door.
BOUNCE BOUNCE.

Next he bounced it off the floor.

BOUNCE BOUNCE.

Then he bounced it off his dad's
head.

BOUNCE BOUNCE.

OWW!

"Don't do that, Little Blue,"
yelled his dad, rubbing his sore
head.

"Sorry, Dad, it was an accident,"
said Little Blue, and picked up
his ball.

He went right to the other end
of the upturned boat, well away
from his dad, and began to play
with his ball again.

First he bounced it off his feet.

BOUNCE BOUNCE.

6

Next he bounced it off his beak.

BOUNCE BOUNCE.

Then he bounced it off his mum's
best vase.

BOUNCE BOUNCE.

CRASH!

"Don't do that, Little Blue,"
sighed his mum, picking up
the pieces.
"Sorry, Mum, it was an accident,"
said Little Blue, and picked up
his ball.

"Why don't you go outside
and play with your ball?"
said his mum and dad.
Little Blue looked out of the
window. It was still raining.

PLOP PLIP **PLOP, PLOP** PLIP **PLOP.**
"I'll try out my rain chant
again," he said. "Then maybe
the rain will go away."

And he chanted…

"RAIN RAIN GO AWAY, THEN
I CAN GO OUT AND PLAY."

PLOP PLIP **PLOP, PLOP** PLIP **PLOP.**

The rain didn't go away.

At that moment there was

a knock on the door. Little Blue

opened it.

"Hi, Little Blue," said his friend,
Rocky, the rockhopper penguin.
"Want to come out and play?"
"But it's raining," said Little
Blue. "We'll get wet."
"Let's go swimming then," said
Rocky. "And we'll get wet
anyway."
"Good idea," said Little Blue.
"I'll take my ball."

Little Blue and Rocky waddled
down to the ocean.

First they played water tennis
and batted the ball to each other
with their flippers.

Then they played water football
and flipped the ball to each other
with their feet.

They were just about to play
a good game of water cricket
when two dark triangular shapes
appeared in the water...
"Oh no," said Little Blue.
"It's the sharks, Fick and Fin.
And I think they've spotted us!"

They had.

They swam a little closer.

"Do you see what I see, Fick?"
said Fin.

"I see the sea, Fin," said Fick.

"Apart from that, Fick," said Fin.

"Let me see..." said Fick.

15

"Oh, I know. I see a little blue penguin and a little rockhopper penguin, Fin."

"You know what that means, Fick?" asked Fin.

"It means there are a lot of penguins round here," said Fick.

"It means LUNCH, you idiot," said Fin. "Let's get them!"

They turned and headed towards
Little Blue and Rocky, teeth
bared and ready.

"SHARK ATTACK, SHARK
ATTACK!" yelled Little Blue.
"Quick, Rocky, dive down
through the seaweed tunnels.
They're too narrow for Fick and
Fin to follow us through."

They dived down. Just in time!

SNAP SNAP!

"Where did they go?" said Fick, snapping his jaws on a long piece of seaweed. "This doesn't taste like penguin."

"That's because it's seaweed, Banana Head," said Fin.

"The penguins have escaped!"

"Actually, I quite like seaweed..." said Fick and ate some more.

Little Blue and Rocky swam
through the seaweed tunnels.
It was scary in there. Big eyes
blinked at them from black holes.
Big claws nipped at them from
black rocks. And there was LOTS
of seaweed.

Slippy seaweed, sloppy seaweed,
slimy seaweed. It clung to the
walls. It hung from the roof.
It curled itself round and round
the penguins as they swam past.

Little Blue and Rocky were glad
when they came up on the other
side. They were covered in
seaweed, but safe.
They waved to Fick and Fin.

"Bye bye, Fick," called Rocky.

"Bye bye, Fin," called Little Blue.

"Bye bye to our lunch," said Fick and Fin and swam away muttering.

Little Blue and Rocky swam
ashore to where Joey, the little
kangaroo, was waiting.

"Hi guys," said Joey. "You've
been in the seaweed tunnels,
I see. I wish I could go down
there."

"No you don't," said Rocky.

"They're scary," said Little Blue.

"Can I play ball with you, then?"
said Joey.

"Yes," said Little Blue. "But where
can we play? My mum and dad
don't like me playing indoors, and
Fick and Fin are out in the bay."

"Come and play in the parkland,"
said Joey. "There's plenty of
shelter under the trees. We'll be
out of the rain there."

"Or I could try my rain chant again," said Little Blue. "Then maybe the rain will go away." And he chanted...

"RAIN RAIN GO AWAY,
THEN WE CAN STAY OUT
AND PLAY."

PLOP PLIP **PLOP, PLOP** PLIP **PLOP.**

The rain didn't go away.

So they went to the parkland.
Little Blue and Rocky had to hop
very fast to keep up with Joey.
They found a dry spot
underneath the trees and
began to play with the ball.

Joey dribbled it with his feet.
Rocky tapped it with his beak,
and Little Blue whacked it so
hard with his flippers, it flew
right out from the trees and
bounced off a large rock on
the edge of the parkland.

"OW," said the large rock and
uncurled itself and lifted its head.

"Oh no," said Little Blue. "I've
bounced the ball off Big Grey!"
"And he's there with his mob,"
said Rocky. "What shall we do?"
"Run!" said Joey.

But it was too late. Big Grey and
his mob thundered up and
surrounded the three friends.

"What have we here?"

said Big Grey.

"Looks like two penguins and

a little Joey," said his mob.

"I can see that," said Big Grey.

"And what were you three

doing?"

34

"We were just playing with the
ball, Big Grey," said Little Blue.
"You were just playing at hitting
ME with the ball," said Big Grey.
"He was, Big Grey," said his mob.
"We saw him."

Little Blue tried to be brave.
"I'm sorry I hit you, Big Grey,"
he said.

"It was an accident. Can I have
my ball back, please?"
"No," said Big Grey, "but I tell
you what you CAN have."
"What?" said Little Blue.
"A dip in the ocean!" said Big Grey.

And he and his mob picked up
the three friends, carried them
to the ocean and threw them in.

"Have a good swim," they
shouted and ran off kicking
the ball.

"NOW what are we going to do?"
asked Rocky and Joey.
"We're soaked, it's raining and
we've no ball to play with.
Perhaps we should just go home."

"No, wait," said Little Blue.
"I have an idea. We'll go and
visit my Grandpa Pen."

Grandpa Pen was having a quiet snooze in the corner of the big old barn where he lived when Little Blue and his friends arrived.

"Hello, Grandpa Pen," said Little
Blue. "Can we come and visit you?
It's raining outside and we can't
play with our ball anymore
because Big Grey and his mob
have taken it."

"Come in, come in," said Grandpa Pen. "I was just having a nice dream about football. Or was it cricket, or tennis? Come to think of it, I might still have an old ball somewhere. I could let you play with it in here, out of the rain, if you like?"

"Oh, that would be great, Grandpa Pen," said Little Blue.

"But there is one condition,"
said Grandpa Pen.

"I know," said Little Blue. "That I
don't hit you on the head with it."

"No, that's not it," said Grandpa
Pen.

"That I don't break your best vase
with it?" said Little Blue.

"No, that's not it either,"
said Grandpa Pen.

"I give up," said Little Blue.

"What is it?"

"That you let me have a game too," said Grandpa Pen. "I haven't had a good game of football, or cricket, or tennis in years!"